Michael Hall

Red

A Crayon's Story

As told by me!

GREENWILLOW BOOKS

An Imprint of HarperCollins Publishers

He was red

But he wasn't very good at it.

Oh dear.

His teacher thought
he needed more practice

I'll draw
a red
strawberry,
then you
draw a red
strawberry.

You can
do this.
Really!

But he couldn't, really.

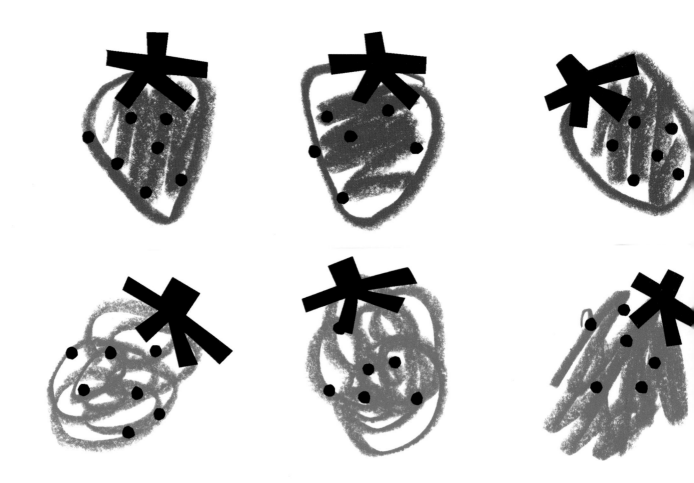

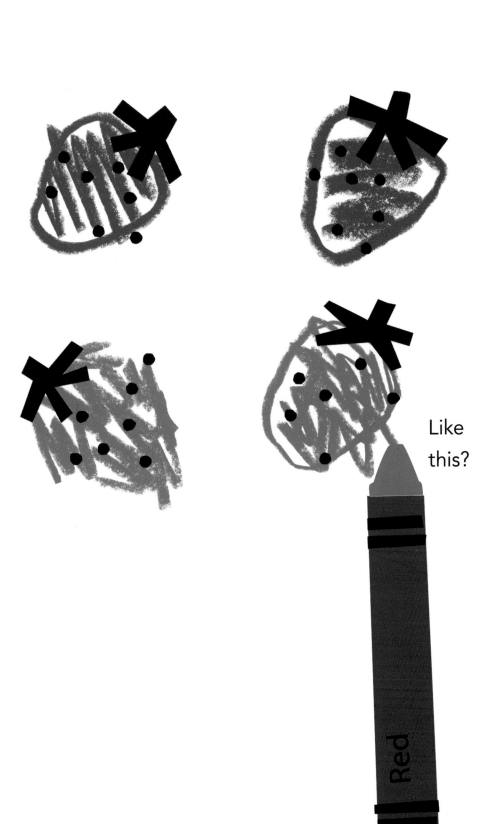

Like
this?

Oh my!
Let's try
again.

Red

Scarlet

His mother thought he needed
to mix with other colors.

Why don't
you two
go out
and draw
a nice,
round
orange.

Olive

A really
big one.

A really
orange
one!

Yellow

Red

But they made
a big greenish one.

Yuck!

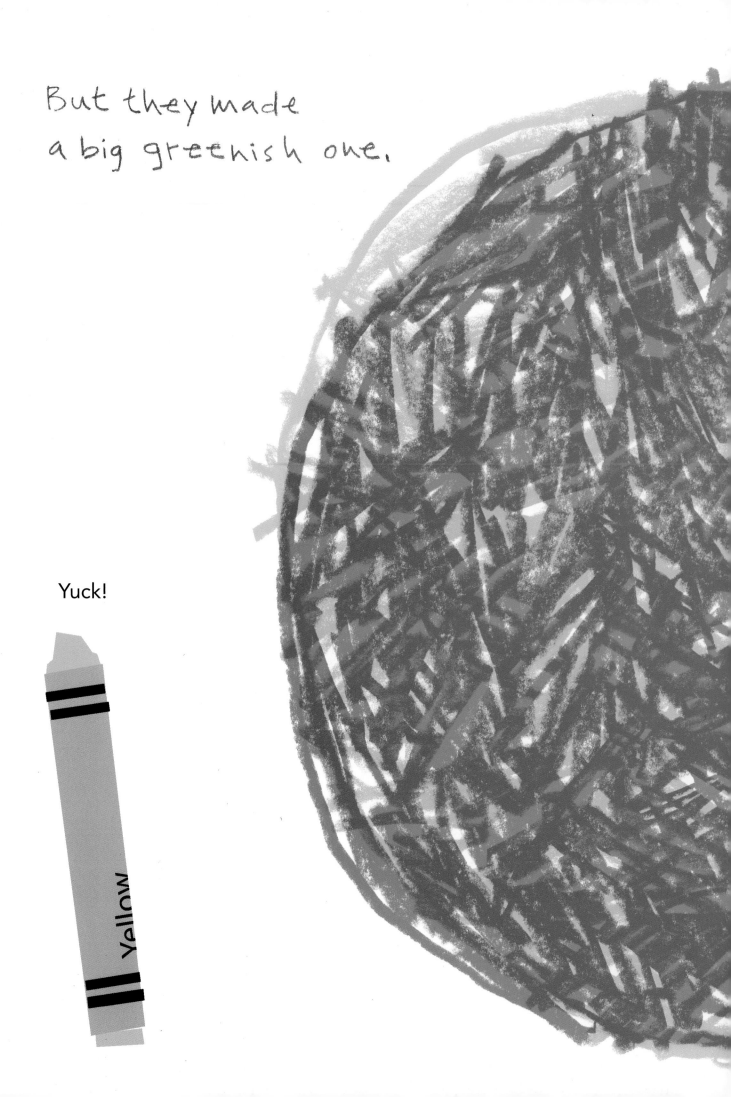

Oops.

His grandparents thought
he wasn't warm enough

Your
class is
making
self-
portraits
for
parents'
night.
Wear this
warm
red scarf.

Nice!
It's so
you!

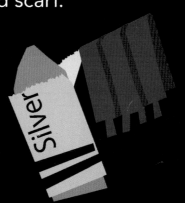

Red

Gray

Silver

But it so wasn't.

Red

orange

Oh,
dear
me.

Olive

Silver

Gray

Everyone seemed to have something to say

Sometimes
I wonder
if he's really
red at all.

Don't
be silly.
It says
red on
his label.

He came
that way
from the
factory.

Frankly,
I don't
think
he's very
bright.

Amber

Hazelnut

Cocoa Bean

Fuchsia

Well,
I think
he's lazy.

Right!
He's got
to press
harder.

Really
apply
himself!

Give
him
time.
He'll
catch
on.

Of
course
he
will.

Grape

Army Green

Steel Gray

Sunshine

Sea Green

But he didn't catch on.

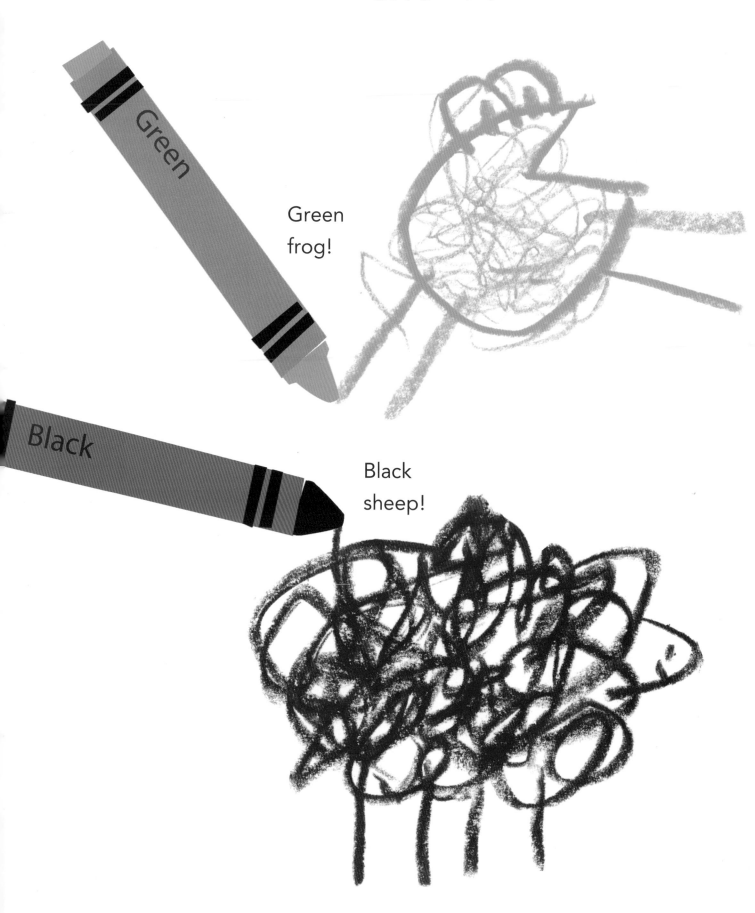

Green
frog!

Black
sheep!

Brown
cow!

Red . . .
aaack!

North Palm Beach Library

All the art supplies
wanted to help.

The masking tape thought
he was broken inside.

This will
help hold you
together.

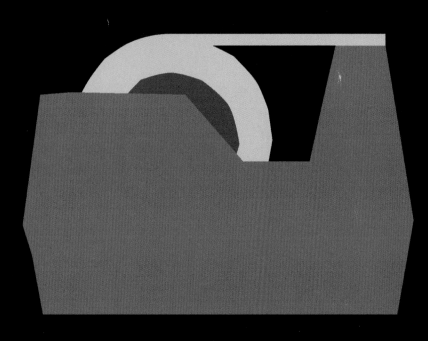

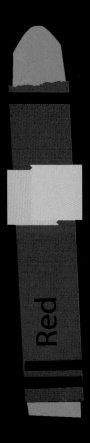

One day, he met a new friend,

Will
you
make
a blue
ocean
for my
boat?

I can't.
I'm red.

Will
you
try?

So he did.

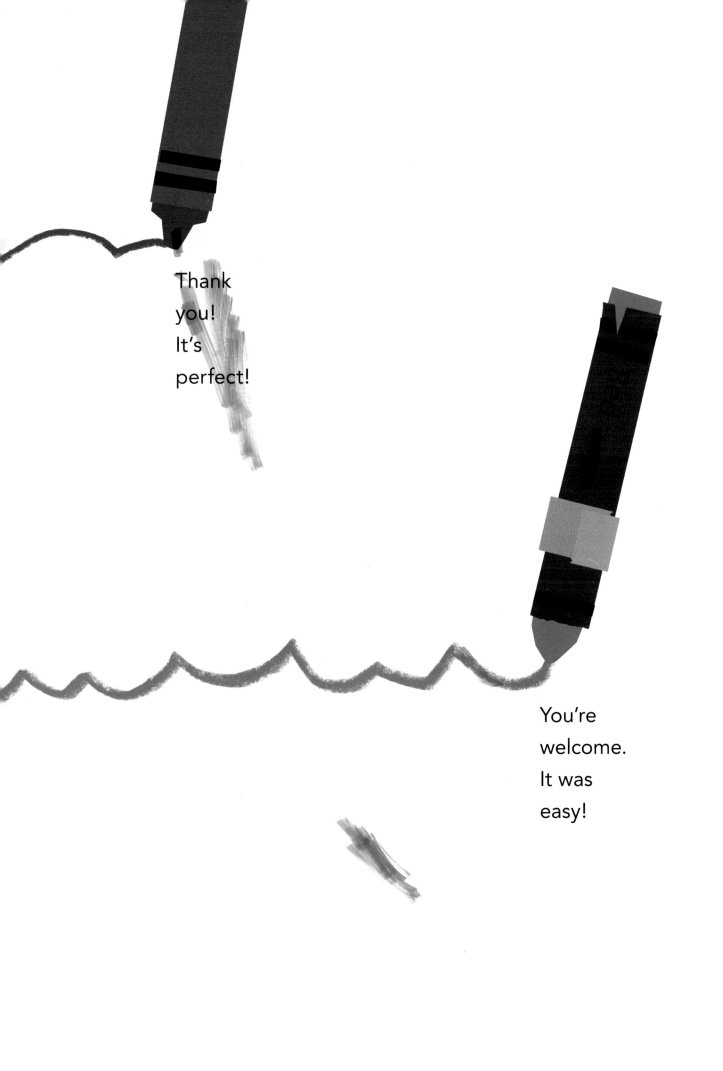

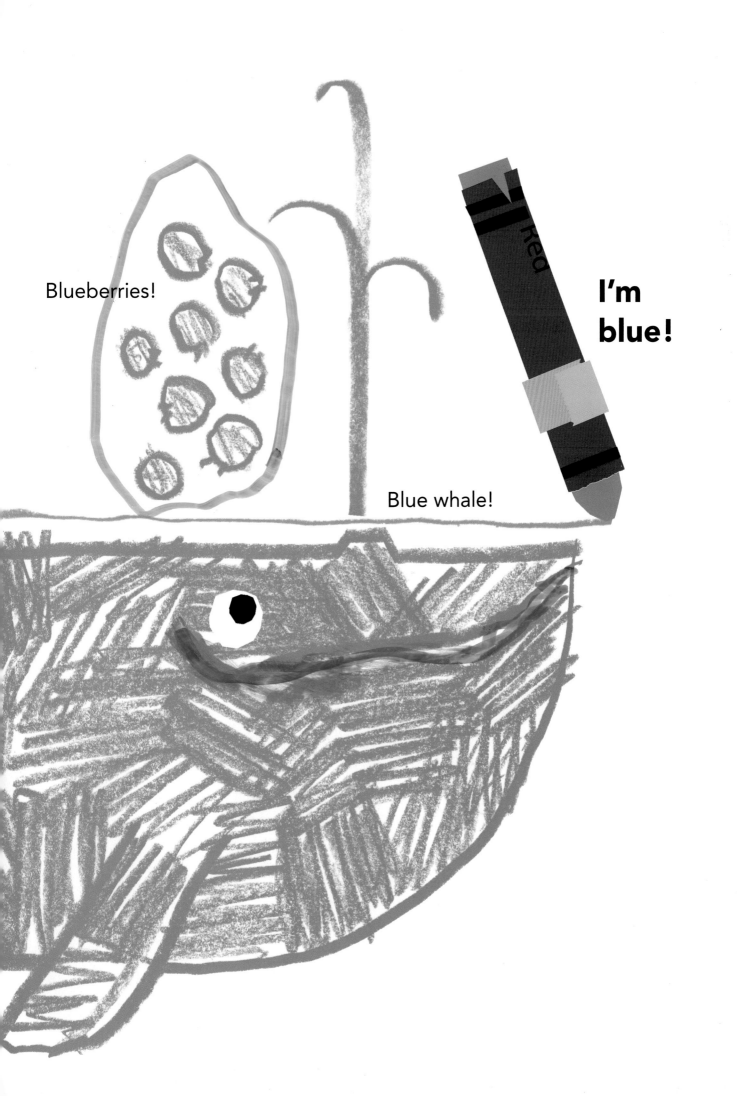

He was ~~red~~ blue.
And everyone was talking.

His
blue
ocean
really
lifted
me.

Who
could
have
known
he was
blue?

I
always
said
he
was
blue.

It
was
obvious!

All
of
his
work
makes
me
happy.

My
son
is
brilliant!

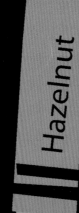

Olive

Amber

Hazelnut

Cocoa Bean

Berry

Sea Green

His
blue
strawberries
are my
favorites.

Brown

He's
so
intense.

Apple Gre

I'm
going
to make
a green
lizard
with him.
A really
big
one.

Yellow

I hear
he's
working
on a
huge
new
project.

Gray

He's
really
reaching
for
the
sky.

Scarlet

And he really was!

For
Debra

For information
address

HarperCollins
Children's
Books,

a division of
HarperCollins
Publishers,

195 Broadway,
New York,
NY 10007.

www.
harpercollins
childrens.com

The art consists
of digitally
combined and
colored
crayon drawings
and cut paper.

The text type is
16-point
Avenir Light.

Library of
Congress
Cataloging-
in-Publication
Data

Hall, Michael,
(date) author,
illustrator.

Red:
a crayon's story /
Michael Hall.
pages cm
"Greenwillow
Books."

Summary:
Red's
factory-applied
label
clearly says
that he is red,
but despite
the best efforts
of his teacher,
fellow crayons
and art supplies,
and family
members,
he cannot
seem to do
anything right
until a new friend
offers a fresh
perspective.

ISBN
978-0-06-225207-4
(trade bdg.)

ISBN
978-0-06-225209-8
(lib. bdg.)

[1. Color—Fiction.
2. Identity—Fiction.
3. Crayons—Fiction.]
I. Title.

PZ7.H1472Red 2015
[E]—dc23 2014010834

15 16 17 18 19 PC
10 9 8 7 6 5 4 3

First Edition

Greenwillow Books